S0-ARO-300

The Fearsome, Frightening, Ferocious BOX

Frances Watts & David Legge

ABC
Books

For Barbara Mobbs, who doesn't scare easily

To learn more about who's hiding in the box visit franceswatts.com/box

  The ABC 'Wave' device and the 'ABC For Kids' device are trademarks of the Australian Broadcasting Corporation and are used under licence by HarperCollins*Publishers* Australia.

First published in Australia in 2013
This edition published in 2014
by HarperCollins*Children's Books*
a division HarperCollins*Publishers* Australia Pty Limited
ABN 36 009 913 517
harpercollins.com.au

Text copyright © Frances Watts 2013
Illustrations copyright © David Legge 2013

The rights of Frances Watts and David Legge to be identified as the author and illustrator of this work have been asserted by them in accordance with the *Copyright Amendment (Moral Rights) Act 2000*.

HarperCollins*Publishers*
Level 13, 201 Elizabeth Street, Sydney NSW 2000, Australia
Unit D1, 63 Apollo Drive, Rosedale, Auckland 0632, New Zealand

National Library of Australia Cataloguing-in-Publication entry:

Watts, Frances.
    The fearsome, frightening, ferocious box / Frances Watts;
    illustrator, David Legge.
    ISBN: 978 0 7333 3270 8 (pbk.)
    Boxes–Juvenile fiction.
    Legge, David, 1963–
    Australian Broadcasting Corporation.
A823.4

Cover and internal design by Matt Stanton, HarperCollins Design Studio
Typesetting by Alicia Freile, Tango Media
Colour reproduction by Graphic Print Group, Adelaide
Printed and bound in China by RR Donnelley on 128gsm Matt Art

This work is copyright. Apart from any use as permitted under the *Copyright Act 1968*, no part may be reproduced, copied, scanned, stored in a retrieval system, recorded, or transmitted, in any form or by any means, without the prior written permission of the publisher.

No one saw it arrive.
No one knew where it came from.
No one knew what was inside.

The first to come across the box was a curious monkey.

'I wonder what it could be?' said Monkey. 'I'll open it.'

But then the box began to moan ...

I hide beneath the slimy weeds,
Which grow in muddy bogs;
Concealed among the rotting reeds,
I float among the logs.
My teeth are sharp, my jaws are wide...
Perhaps you'd like to see inside?

Open the box, if you dare,
But danger lies within: beware!

But which creature am I? Your eyes will play tricks.

In each scene you search, I could be one of six ...

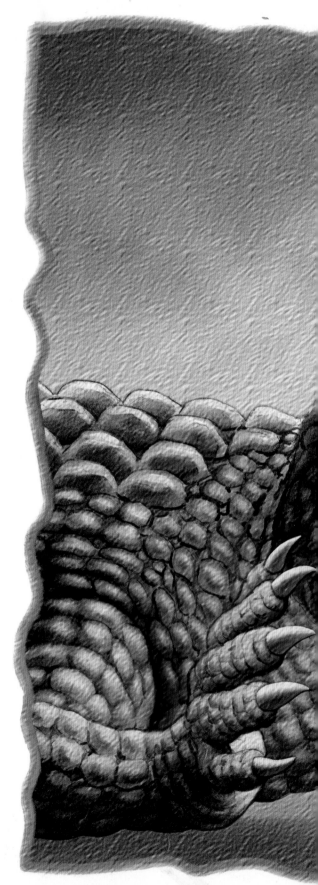

'Maybe I won't open the box,' said Monkey
to Crocodile, who had come up behind.
'There's some kind of horrible beast inside!'

'Ha! It can't be more horrible than me,' said
Crocodile. 'Stand aside, Scaredy-Monkey,
and *I'll* open the box.'

But as Crocodile stomped towards it,
the box began to groan...

In each scene you search, I could be one of six ...

But which creature am I? Your eyes will play tricks.

I drift upon a **freezing** floe
And never feel the cold;
A mountain moving through the snow,
I'm **monstrous** to behold,
With whiskers and wrinkles and layers of fat —
Come too close and I'll **squash** you flat!

Open the box, if you dare,
But danger lies within: **beware!**

'On second thoughts, I won't open
the box,' said Crocodile to Walrus,
who had come up behind.
'It's hiding a hideous creature!'

'Hideous? I'll show you hideous!' said Walrus.
'See you later, Crocodile. *I'll* open the box.'

But as Walrus waddled towards it,
the box began to croak ...

But which creature am I? Your eyes will play tricks.

In each scene you search, I could be one of six ...

I circle above in scorching air,
With **beady** eyes and a hungry stare,
Waiting for some tasty snack
To lose its footing on the track.
If you should hear a dreadful **screech**,
It's too late to **run** — you're in my reach.

Open the box, if you dare,
But danger lies within: **beware!**

'Perhaps I shouldn't open the box,' said Walrus to Vulture,
who had come up behind. 'The thing inside sounds fearsome!'

'Fearsome is my middle name,' said Vulture.
'Watch out, Walrus, *I'll* open the box.'

But as Vulture flapped towards it, the box began to roar ...

Where you see a river racing
Down a rocky mountainside,
By the torrent I'll be pacing;
There's no place for you to hide.

Scramble over slippery stones
Or face me, if you're brave,
But with just one blow I'll break your bones
And drag you to my cave.

Open the box, if you dare,
But danger lies within: beware!

In each scene you search, I could be one of six ...

But which creature am I? Your eyes will play tricks.

'You know, opening the box is probably not a good idea,' said Vulture to Bear, who had come up behind. 'Not with that frightening brute inside.'

'I'll be doing the frightening around here,' said Bear.
'Vamoose, Vulture! *I'll* open the box.'

But as Bear lumbered towards it, the box began to $grow|$ ...

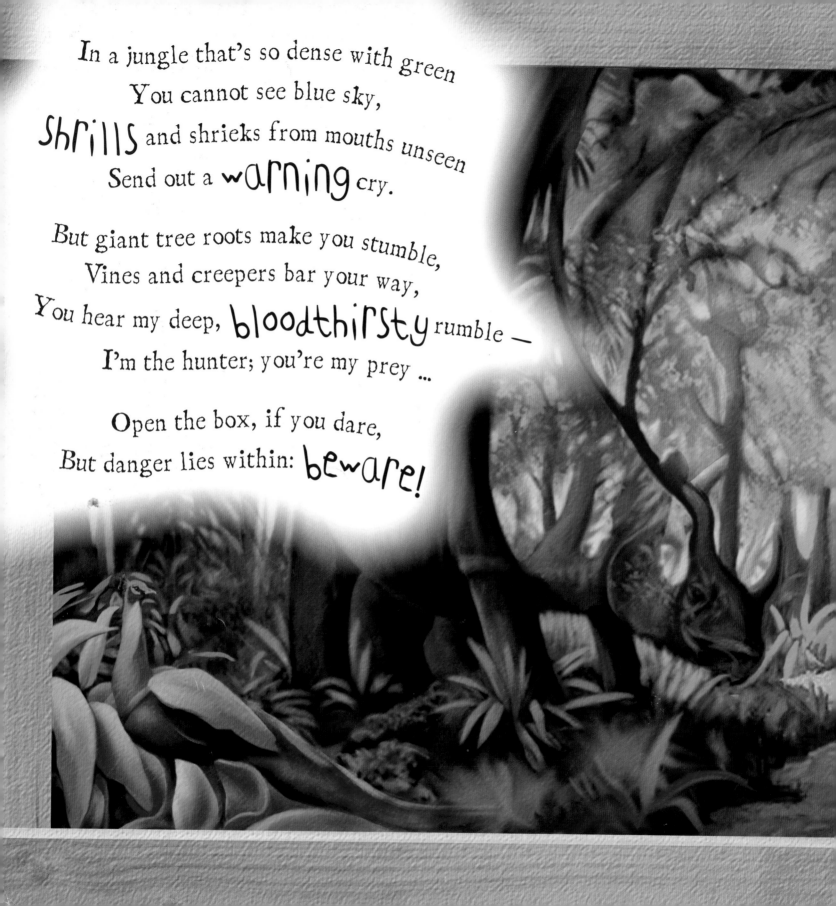

In a jungle that's so dense with green
You cannot see blue sky,
Shrills and shrieks from mouths unseen
Send out a warning cry.

But giant tree roots make you stumble,
Vines and creepers bar your way,
You hear my deep, bloodthirsty rumble —
I'm the hunter; you're my prey ...

Open the box, if you dare,
But danger lies within: beware!

'After careful consideration, I've decided not to open the box,'
said Bear to Tiger, who had come up behind.
'A ferocious fiend is about to pounce!'

'Ferocious, you say? I laugh in the face of ferocious,' said Tiger.
'Back off, Bear, *I'll* open the box.'

But as Tiger stalked towards it, the box began to wail ...

In each scene you search, I could be one of six ...

But which creature am I? Your eyes will play tricks.

Through the woods a thin mist drifts
Round twisting trunk and bending tree.
As darkness falls a shadow shifts,
But what it is you can't quite see.

It's drawing nearer, on the prowl,
You feel its breath upon your brow
And hear its haunting hunting howl —
There's no one who can save you now ...

Open the box, if you dare,
But danger lies within: beware!

'I've changed my mind about opening the box,' said Tiger to Wolf, who had come up behind. 'There's something truly terrifying inside!'

'No one's more terrifying than Mr Wolf,' said Wolf. 'Look and learn, Tiger. *I'll* open the box.'

But as Wolf loped towards it,
the box **cried**:

Open the box and I tell you true,
It's the last thing you will ever do!

Open the box and I will attack,
I'm warning you now: get back! Get back!

Open the box, if you dare,
But danger lies within: beware!

Beware!

'Er, actually,' said Wolf, 'I don't think I'll open the box after all ...'

'Wait a minute,' said Monkey, who was still curious. 'We're a pretty horrible, hideous, fearsome, frightening, ferocious and terrifying bunch of animals. Surely we're a match for the beast in the box! Let's open it together on the count of three.'